Written by Raphaëlle Brice
Illustrated by Claude and Denise Millet

Specialist adviser: Robert Press,
Botanical Consultant

ISBN 1 85103 010 7
First published 1986 in the United Kingdom by
Moonlight Publishing Ltd,
131 Kensington Church Street, London W8

The Potato

American Indians
first discovered potatoes...

Potato:

an Indian name, from South America where they were first discovered.

Potatoes are never eaten raw.

There are hundreds of ways of cooking potatoes: roast, mashed, fried, in soup, in salads...

When potatoes are cooked in the oven with their skins left on, 'in their jackets', they go soft and fluffy inside. Sliced up and deep-fried in oil, they become crisp and brown. Which is the way you like them best?

In olden days, in winter, children going to school would tuck a hot baked potato in each pocket. They kept their hands warm and carried their lunch at the same time!

The flower

A potato is not a root
like a carrot; it's
not a bulb like an
onion; it's not a
fruit like rhubarb.

A potato is a tuber.
It is a kind of swelling in the stems
underground. Potato plants do have a
fruit, which looks just like
a tiny green tomato,
but be careful!
Potato fruit
is poisonous.

The fruit

Jerusalem artichokes (1) and sweet potatoes (2)
are tubers; yams (3) and manioc (4) are roots.

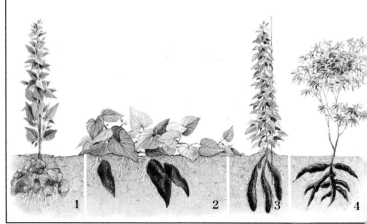

One potato, planted, may give fifteen to twenty new potatoes.

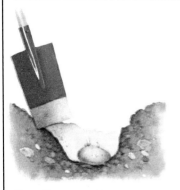

In the spring, a potato from last year's crop is planted in the soil. A shoot appears, grows and pushes up through the ground. It feeds on the goodness stored up in the old potato. Roots develop and then begin to swell out into tiny potatoes.

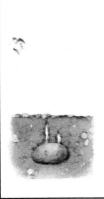

The old potato shrivels up as the plant develops.

A small mound
of earth is heaped up round the base of
the plant. This shelters the young
potatoes as they grow in the dark soil. If
they do catch the light
they go green and
can't be eaten. In
the autumn the
leaves wither.
This is the
signal that the
potatoes are full-grown with
strong skins.
They are
ready to
harvest.

Where do potatoes come from?

Very long ago, the Incas, in Peru in South America, grew small potatoes to feed themselves and their animals.

The Spanish discovered America, and the potato.

After Christopher Columbus discovered America, General Pizarro and his soldiers set out to conquer Peru. They came across Indians who ate a vegetable which they called 'batata': the potato. When the Spaniards sailed home, in about 1570, they carried crates of potatoes on board, the first to be seen in Europe.

Like the Incas, the Indians in Peru today dry their potatoes so that they keep for years. First they tread them to press out the water, then they leave them out at night to freeze.

This strange foreign vegetable was not popular at first.

In the seventeenth century, peasants preferred to feed potatoes to their pigs rather than eat them themselves.

Sir Walter Raleigh brought the first potato to England.

Parmentier plays a trick.

But Parmentier, a French scientist, knew potatoes are good for you. So, to make them popular, he pretended they were very precious and set guards round the fields. People, eager to find out what made them so special, crept in and stole the potatoes. They tasted good.

Parmentier

Harvesting potatoes

Before farm machines were invented, people had to harvest potatoes by hand. They dug them up and left them to dry i the fields before sorting them out. Any that had been damaged were fed to the animals, some were kept for selling or

eating on the farm, and some were kept for next year's crop. For a long while, though, potatoes were seen simply as poor people's food. Only in the last hundred years have they become really popular.

The Colorado beetle is the potato's worst enemy.

The female beetle can lay 2500 eggs, which in five or six weeks hatch out into larvae, which then grow up and lay eggs The larvae are so eager to eat that thirty

of them can devour a whole potato plant in a week. Worms, slugs, millipedes, all eat potatoes too.

Potato damaged
by (1) larvae and
(2) wireworm.

Luckily, wasps,
ladybirds and pigeons
all like eating the larvae
of Colorado beetles.

Potatoes have other enemies as well as animals and insects.

Potato blight

A tiny fungus which dries out the leaves of the plant and turns the tubers to dust. It can easily destroy a whole crop. That is what happened in Ireland in the nineteenth century. With nothing to eat, thousands of Irish peasants set out to try their luc in America.

Today there are chemicals which are sprayed onto the crops by machines. They kill the insects and weeds which harm the potatoes, and they control potato blight.

Weeds can choke potato plants.

Today potatoes are entirely harvested by machine.

Machines can dig up the potatoes and separate them from stones and clods of earth.

A sorting machine grades the potatoes into several categories, depending on their size. Mis-shapen and green potatoes are picked out by hand so that they do not go to be sold.

A sorting machine

Have you seen how many different kinds of potato there are for sale in the shops?

If they are stored somewhere dry and dark, such as a cellar, potatoes will keep for up to a year.

Do you like eating new potatoes?
New potatoes are picked while the plant is still growing. Their skins are very thin, and hardly protect them. New potatoes are sweet and delicious to eat, but cannot be stored.

Sometimes potatoes are stored in 'clamps', shelters made of straw and soil to keep out the frost.

Corn   Grown particularly in Mexico, Peru, the United States and Europe.

Wheat   Grown in Europe, the United States and Russia.

Millet   Grown above all in Africa, because it can survive the hot, dry climate.

Rice   Grown in 'paddy-fields' all over Asia.

In some countries,
they eat cereals
instead of potatoes
at nearly every meal.

Corn is eaten in South
America; it is eaten
roasted. Pancakes
called 'tortillas' are
made with cornflour.

Wheat is eaten nearly
everywhere in the world;
the flour is used for
bread and cakes.
In North Africa a
special dish called
'couscous' is made from
ground wheat mixed with
meat and vegetables.

Millet is eaten in
Africa, ground into
flour and made into
porridge and dumplings.

Rice is eaten in
Asia at nearly every
meal, from a bowl
with chopsticks.

Crisps, chips and precooked potatoes

Sometimes, instead of preparing potatoes yourself, you may buy them ready for you to cook. They can be bought as powder to make into mashed potato, or chips which only need to be fried or put in the oven. Or just crisps, in a packet.

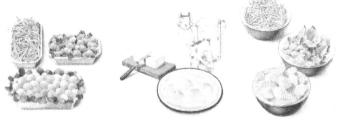

To make potato powder, the potatoes have been boiled, mashed, dried in a hot-air machine, and then powdered. When you use it at home, all you have to do is add hot water or milk, and perhaps a dab of butter.

There are special kinds of potato which are grown specially for the production of **starch.** This is a white powder which, because it is smooth, absorbent, and gluey, can be used for all sorts of things:

there is starch in sauces, soups, cakes, blancmanges, and ice creams,

in synthetic fibres, in glue, in some medicines, in electric batteries,

in cardboard, in paper, and even in disposable nappies for babies.

Some people's work is studying potatoes.

They try to create new and better varieties. Taking the pollen from one potato flower, they place it carefully on the flower of a potato of another kind: this is called "cross-fertilisation". If one potato is good at resisting disease, and another tastes nice, by combining them scientists try to breed a potato which resists disease and tastes nice. At first, these new kinds of potato are grown in test-tubes, then the young plants are looked after in sheltered greenhouses until they are strong enough to grow outside.

You can make potatoes work for you.

To make a potato print, cut a potato in half. Draw on your design with a pencil (simple, clear shapes are best), then cut round it with a knife. Your design should stand out in relief.

To make a print, take the lid of a jar and layer the bottom with blotting-paper or cotton-wool, then soak this pad with ink or paint. Next, take your potato and press it, face down, onto the pad, and then onto the piece of paper you want to print. You can make patterns for yourself, or on cards and gifts for your friends.

For this recipe, you will need:

4 big potatoes   8 eggs    50g butter   salt   pepper

Eggs in their nests

Set the oven to a fairly high temperature (gas mark 7, 400°F).

Wash the potatoes and set them to bake in the oven for one and a half hours.

Then melt the butter in a saucepan.

Take the potatoes out of the oven, cut them in half and scoop a little out of the middle of each one to make a nest. Lay them in a baking-dish, pour a little butter into each one, and then break an egg onto each nest. Add salt and pepper and put back into the oven until the eggs are cooked.

For this recipe, you will need:

potato
powder

½ litre water

3 eggs

salt

pepper

100g grated
gruyère cheese

butter

Potato soufflé

Set the oven to a medium temperature.
Butter a 7″ soufflé dish. Mix the potato
powder with the water (nearly boiling)
and a pinch of salt. Separate the eggs.
Add the egg yolks, butter, grated cheese,
salt and pepper to the potato mixture.
Beat the egg whites until stiff and fold
them into the mixture. Place in the dish,
and bake in the oven for about
40 minutes.
Serve
immediately,
while it is still
beautifully
risen.

Both these dishes are good with salad.

Index